I0692598

Fennings Taylor

Thomas D'Arcy McGee

sketch of his life and death

Fennings Taylor

Thomas D'Arcy McGee
sketch of his life and death

ISBN/EAN: 9783337387907

Printed in Europe, USA, Canada, Australia, Japan

Cover: Foto ©Andreas Hilbeck / pixelio.de

More available books at **www.hansebooks.com**

THOS. D'ARCY McGEE:

SKETCH

OF HIS

LIFE AND DEATH,

By FENNINGS TAYLOR,

WITH A

LIFE-SIZED PORTRAIT BY W. NOTMAN.

———— • ————

MONTREAL:

PRINTED BY JOHN LOVELL, ST. NICHOLAS STREET.

1868.

THE HONORABLE THOMAS D'ARCY MCGEE

OF MONTREAL.

HAD the Honorable Thomas D'Arcy McGee lived in the middle of the sixth century he would very probably have been a member, and a very distinguished one too, of that all-powerful " Bardic Order," before whose awful anger, Mr. McGee informs us in his History of Ireland, " Kings trembled and warriors succumbed in superstitious dread." This influential order, we are elsewhere told, were " the Editors, Professors, Registrars, and Record Keepers" of those early days, the makers and masters of public opinion, whose number in the Provinces of Meath and Ulster alone, in the reign of King Hugh the Second, exceeded twelve hundred. Although the subject of our sketch may neither be a prophet, nor the son of a prophet, it is not improbable that, could we trace his genealogy aright, we might discover that the trunk of his family tree is rooted and grounded in poetic earth; for his intellectual life derives no slight nourishment from the poet's heritage,—imagination and fancy. Mr. McGee's ancestors hailed originally from Ulster. It is therefore probable he descends through them from the imposing commonwealth of bards to which we have referred, and that his scholar-like forefathers must be looked for among the twelve hundred whom King Hugh impeached, but who were upheld and defended by that illustrious travel-stained saint, who, moved by a love of letters, and a schoolman's sympathies, had to that end, expressly journeyed from his sea-girt home at Icolumkill. On referring to one of the larger and more perfect maps of Ireland, and looking closely along the north-eastern coast, we shall perceive situated sea-ward off the shore of

Antrim, in the province of Ulster, and within the ancient Barony of Belfast, a small islet which bears the name of " Island Magee." This little sea-washed speck contained, according to one of the latest, if not the latest topographical survey, about seven thousand acres of the finest land in the northern part of the kingdom. Moreover, in 1837 it was peopled by no less than two thousand six hundred and ten inhabitants. In the early times, the lordship of the Island was vested in the great Ulster family of O'Neil, from whom it passed in the sixteenth century to the Macdonalds of the Antrim Glens, and in the seventeenth, by the fortune of arms, to the Chichesters, Earls of Belfast and Marquises of Donegal. From this small Island, for which the original tenants are said to have paid the annual rental of " two goshawks and a pair of gloves," (which, by the way, may have been considered enough, since, to an incredibly recent period, the Island was imagined by its inhabitants to be a theatre of sorcery,)—their descendants were almost exterminated, and wholly expelled by a force of covenanters at the time when the memorable Munroe was commander of the Parliamentary armies in Ireland. Three only of those who bore the name of Magee were said to have escaped to the mainland, and from one of those three, who we suspect must have appropriated more than his share of the sorcery, the subject of our sketch accounts himself to have directly descended.

Without dwelling further on the facts and incidents of his remote ancestry, we may mention that the Honorable Thomas D'Arcy McGee is the second son of the late Mr. James McGee, of Wexford, and of Dorcas Morgan, his wife. He was born at Carlingford, in the County of Louth, and we are enabled to add, on the 13th of April, 1825. The name of " D'Arcy," by which Mr. McGee is conventionally known, is, we have understood, derived from his godfather Mr. Thomas D'Arcy, a gentlemen who resided in the neighborhood of Carlingford, and, as we may infer, a personal friend of the family. Of his parents Mr. McGee is accustomed to speak with filial affection and becoming reverence, for he was early taught to " honor his father and his mother." But for the memory of the latter, whom he lost at a very early age, if we may publish in this place the observations of his most cherished friends, he entertains feelings of tender and enthusiastic admiration. Such feelings appear to be almost divinely wrought, and, like threads of gold, they beautify as well as strengthen the purest fibres of our nature. On the mind of Mr. McGee they have exerted the gentle influence of poetry as well as the holy one of love. Separate qualities, such as duty and pride, obedience and devotion, when looked at through the lens of his memory, cease to be distinct. All his recollections of his mother, though differently colored, nevertheless meet and blend harmoniously, like the soft hues of the rainbow, as in the hush of evening they silently melt in a sea of light.

No doubt there were strong intellectual affinities between the mother and her son; and this sympathetic attraction created an indelible impression on the heart of the latter. The intellectual charts of the two minds were, we are inclined to think, marked with not dissimilar lines; bold and deeply drawn in the case of the son, they were sketchily traced and delicately shaded in the instance of the mother. The subtle charm of divine poesy seems to have pervaded both; and this spell of fancy and feeling, of imagination and truth, may, in some sort, account for the magnetic attractions which governed the intercourse of the parent and child.

To talk about his mother is, as we have had occasion to observe, a source of unalloyed happiness to her son. As in a holiday in his boyhood, the acids of controversy and the sharp edges of strife give place to expressions tipped with sunshine, when his lips can be beguiled into speaking of what his heart never ceases to feel.

> " My mother! at that holy name
> Within my bosom there's a gush
> Of feeling, which no time can tame,
> A feeling which for years of fame
> I would not, could not crush ! "

According to his recollection of her, the subject of our sketch always alludes to his mother as a person of genius and acquirements, rare in her own or in any other class. She was endowed, as Mr. McGee is accustomed to say, with a fertile imagination as well as a cultivated mind. Nature had given her a sweet voice and an exquisite ear, and the latter prescribed exact laws to the former when, bird-like, the owner thought fit to attune that voice to song. She was fond of music, as well as of its twin sister, poetry. A diligent reader of the best books, she was also an intelligent lover of

the best ballads. She liked especially those of Scotland. The
poetry of common life was in her case no mere figure of speech.
Through all the changes of daily duty there ran a vein of fancy,
which enabled her to brighten the real with the pleasant phantasies
of the ideal, and support the dark cares of the mind on the white
wings of the imagination.

> " Oh whar hae you been a' the day
>   My boy Tammie ! "

were the words with which she usually greeted and welcomed her
favorite child.   In common with her contemporaries, the mothers
of her day, we suspect she had a special liking for Home's tragedy
of Douglas ; and we may perhaps more easily imagine than describe
her sense of pride as she listened to " Tammie's" earliest lesson in
elocution. It is not difficult to see the curly-headed urchin standing
on a table, and in melo-dramatic guise, with precocious effrontery
informing his mother, who knew better, and his mother's friends who
did not believe him, that

> " My name is Norval."

His mother, as we have said, was early removed from him by death.
We will not speak of, since we cannot describe, grief. We may,
however, conjecture, since their natures and intellectual tastes were
identical, that her death was like a severance of himself from himself.
The great tears, however, which no doubt fell upon her grave, were
neither idle nor unavailing tears, for they became as it were so many
cameras through which were reflected the duties, the incidents, and
the obligations of his future life.   Thus at the age of seventeen we
find D'Arcy McGee had passed the shallows where timid youths
bathe and shiver, and had boldly struck out into the deep sea of
duty.   We have no data which will enable us to bridge the time
between his mother's death and his arrival on this continent : but it
is not difficult to suppose that it was filled up in the manner usual
to youth, with the difference only of a greater amount of application
and a higher range of study.   On arriving at Boston, he became
almost immediately connected with the press of that city.   Kind
fortune seemed to befriend him ; for his lot appeared to be cast in,
what was at that time, as perhaps it still is, the intellectnal capital

of the United States—the forcing-house of its fanaticism, and the favored seats of its scholarship. Thus it was that D'Arcy McGee, the youth hungry and thirsty for knowledge and fame, found himself a resident of the New England States capital, with access to the best public libraries on this side of the Atlantic, and within reach of the best public lecturers on literary and scientific subjects. For at that day Emerson, Giles, (the county and countryman of the subject of our sketch,) Whipple, Chapin, and Brownson, lived in that city or in its vicinity. It was moreover the residence of Channing, Bancroft, Eastburn, Prescott, Ticknor, Longfellow, Lowell, Holmes, and others, whose influence should have purified the moral atmosphere, and have made Boston to others, what we suppose it must have been to them, an appreciative and congenial home. It is not difficult to imagine, from what we know and can observe of his mature manhood, that D'Arcy McGee, the impulsive Irish lad, overflowing with exuberant good nature and untiring industry, with his full heart and active brain, soon found his way into meetings where learned men delivered lectures, or among the booksellers, whose shops such celebrities frequented. Neither is it a matter for surprise that he early attracted the notice of several of their number. Opportunities of speaking publicly are by no means uncommon in the United States, and we should imagine that Boston contained a great many nurseries, under different names, where the alphabet of the art could be acquired. Whether the scholar progresses beyond his letters depends very much on the furnishing of his mind. The nerve and knack may be got by practice, but the prime condition,—having something to say,—must spring from exact thought, and severe study. We have every reason to believe that the subject of our sketch, even in his early youth, observed that condition ; but we have no means of knowing where or in what way he acquired the fluent habit of graceful and polished oratory. For since he was enthroned on his mother's tea-table, and declared to listening friends that his name was " Norval," we have been unable to discover any intermediate audience between his select one at Carlingford, and his scientific one at Boston. Strange as it may seem, it is we believe, no less true than strange, that during his sojourn at Boston, between the years 1842 and 1845, when between the ages of seventeen and twenty, he had actually made his mark as a public speaker. Nor was it, we believe, denied that the audacious youth, though contemptuously styled " Greenhorn," and " Paddy-boy," very fairly held his own with men who never were " green" and who had long ceased to be "boys." It may be observed in passing that the " Know-nothing" party, which has since then acquired consistency and influence, was, in its incipient shape, discernible at that day under the name of the Anti-foreign party, a party which Mr. McGee could not do do otherwise than criticise with severity and oppose with vehemence.

At the period we refer to, the " Lyceum System" as it has been termed, spread itself over the New England States. People desired to receive knowledge distilled through the brains of their neighbors. Lecturers were at a premium ; and youth forestalled time by discoursing of wisdom, irrespective of experience. Thus it was that Mr. McGee, with a boy's down on his chin, and with whiskers in embryo, itinerated among our neighbors, and gave them the advantage of listening to a youthful lecturer, discoursing, we must be permitted to think, on aged subjects. What those subjects may have been we cannot conjecture ; but we have little doubt that the reminiscences of Mr. McGee's lecturing life in those days are full of amusing as well as of instructive incident ; for the period is, we think, coeval with a transition phase not only of the Irish, but of the American, mind.

Mixing, as he necessarily must have done, with all sorts and conditions of men, it was impossible that Mr. McGee should not have formed many acquaintances more or less valuable, and some friendships, it may be, beyond price. Among the latter it is his practice to make grateful mention of Mr. Grattan, then Her Majesty's Consul at Boston. Besides a name historically eloquent which he inherited, that gentlemen, it is said, possessed great intellectual acquirements as well as personal gifts. In the latter were included a kindly disposition and a cordial manner. It was therefore natural enough that he should have taken a warm interest in his enthusiastic countryman, and that from the treasury of his own experience he should have given the young writer and lecturer many valuable hints on the style and structure of literary work. Thus it chanced that the wise counsellor and the kind friend meeting in the same person, exerted no inconsiderable influence on the young enthusiast. Mr. Grattan's sympathies fell upon an appreciative mind; for Mr. McGee always speaks of his character with admiration and of his services with gratitude.

A new page in the eventful life of the subject of our sketch was however about to be opened. The obscure lad who had turned his back upon Ierland was about to be beckoned home again by the country he had left. The circumstances, apart from their political significance, were in the highest degree complimentary to one who at the time was not "out of his teens." An article, written by Mr. McGee, on an Irish subject, in a Boston newspaper, having attracted the attention of the late Mr. O'Connell, the former received, early in the year 1845, a very handsome offer from the proprietors of the "Freeman's Journal," a Dublin daily paper, for his editorial services. This proposal he accepted, and hence his personal participation in the Irish politics of the eventful years which commenced then and ended in 1848. Ardent by temperament, and enthusiastic by disposition, it was almost impossible for Mr. McGee to keep within the bounds of moral force which Mr. O'Connell had prescribed, and which the newspaper he served was instructed to advocate. Mr. McGee felt that such fetters galled him, and he became impatient under their restraint. The habit of maintaining his own convictions was, and is, a necessity of his condition. Following the lead of his feelings, he determined at all hazards to associate himself with the more advanced and enthusiastic section of the liberal party, then known by the name of "Young Ireland." This section or *coterie*, for it was scarcely a party, possessed many attractions for such an adherent. Besides the name, and the bright, alluring, misleading quality of youth, which that name symbolized and expressed, the *coterie* was made up of those many-hued forms of intellectual mosaic work which men generally admire and rarely trust; very charming in our sight and very perishable in our service. It was composed, at least at first, almost altogether of young barristers, young doctors, young college men and young journalists, most of them under thirty, and many under twenty-five years of age. Mr. McGee was probably their most youthful member, for when his association with them commenced he was not of age. Of such hot blood was the "Young Ireland" party compounded, that little surprise was occasioned, and none was expressed, when its mischievous revels were broken up by the riot act. If we understand the history of those times aright, the policy of moral force which had guided O'Connell was not, in the first instance, discarded by his younger and more ardent disciples. They wished to accomplish the purpose of "The Liberator," only they desired to shorten the time and accelerate the speed of the operation. They thought that O'Connell was "old and slow." They felt that they were young and active. In their minds the rivalry between age and youth was renewed, provoking the old issues and re-enacting the old results. Keeping in view the great end which they had set themselves to accomplish, they nevertheless sought, in the first instance, to move by literary rather than by political appliances. Accordingly they planned, among other works, a series of stirring shilling volumes for the people, entitled the "Library of Ireland." The famine of 1847 extinguished the enterprize, but not until twenty volumes of this new National Library had been published. Of the above number Mr. McGee was the author of two. One, a series of biographies of illustrious Irishmen of the seventeenth century, and the other a memoir of "Art. McMurrough," a half forgotten Irish king of the fourteenth century. Of course, works published under such circumstances, and forming parts of such a series, would at first, at all events, be well received and widely circulated; but their merits could not have been of a mere evanescent character, for we are credibly informed that now, after a period of twenty years, the books we have mentioned still retain their popularity.

Mr. McGee, if we remember aright, has somewhere said, with respect to the transactions of those times, that "Young Ireland," not content to restore the past, endeavored to re-enact it; not content to write history, tried, to use a familiar phrase of Mr. John Sandfield Macdonald's, to "make it;" and we have little doubt, could we see the intellectual machinery which preceded those events, we should discover that none more than Mr. McGee have assiduously labored to manufacture history.

The *coterie* grew into a confederation of which Mr. McGee was, we believe, the chief promoter and the chosen secretary. It was not without adherents, neither was it without attraction, and especially to the class, a by no means inconsiderable one, whose judgment is controlled by their imagination, and who seem to think that feeling and wisdom are identical qualities. We decline to indicate those transactions by any particular name. We all know that they were failures, and since time tempers judgment, we venture to believe that the actors of that day concur with the critics of the present time in thinking that they were follies. The most stirring among the many impassioned "Songs of the Nation,"—" Who fears to speak of '98"—showed alike the genius, the courage, and the credulity of " Young Ireland" of '48. The Irish politics of fifty years since were no more worthy of recall than was the Irish policy of two hundred years since. Young Ireland should not, we venture to think, have invoked the embarrasing memories of the past, if it wished to make old Ireland new. It was an error in time, an error in judgment, and an error in sense, which, fortunately for all, contained within itself the germ of inevitable failure.

While England, through her press and in her Parliament, scouted the policy and punished its principal exponents, she did not fail very generously to acknowledge the unquestionable talent and out-spoken honesty of that earnest and ill-fated party. We all know what followed. Some of the leaders were sent into penal exile, while others, including the subject of our sketch, found safety in voluntary expatriation. Thus it was that, heated and excited by the strife, angered and disappointed at the issue, Mr. McGee for a second time landed in the United States. As before, his occupations were those of a journalist and a lecturer, for it is his pleasure to live by the sweat of his brain. Between the close of 1848 and the commencement of 1857, he published two newspapers, " The New York Nation," and the " American Celt." It was, of course, natural, all the circumstances considered, that the inclination of his mind should have been violently and from the force of recent discipline, bitterly hostile to the Government of Great Britain. Many will remember, not from the papers themselves, for they had but a small circulation in the Provinces, but from extracts which found a place in several of the Canadian journals, how fiercely and bitterly anti-English his political writings were. But while admitting the exaggerated rancour which characterized his words, it will undoubtedly be allowed that time and the opportunity for closer observation produced their usual influence on his instructed mind. His fierce anger towards Great Britain gradually disappeared. His excited temper, like the evil spirit of the son of Kish, was exorcised, if not by the spell of music, at least by the force of acquired truth and the sense of obvious wrong. The book of remembrance and the book of experience were before him. He could read their letter-press and criticise their illustrations. He could see his country-men under British and his countrymen under American rule. He could look from that picture to this, from Monarchical England to Republican America, and with all the imperfections of the former, he would probably express his judgment of the contrast in the words of the Prince of Denmark, that taken all in all "it was Hyperion to a Satyr."

We could not, even in the cursory sketch which our limited space will permit us to make, pass over in silence Mr. McGee's personal and political career previous to his residence in Canada, for a por-tion of that career was a prelude to, and directly connected with, its more recent sequences amongst ourselves. His occupations during that period were professedly those of an author and lecturer, and only accidentally those of a politician. Those occupations were marked with many errors and crossed with many vicissitudes. Still it must be allowed that if one of his ardent temperament and peculiar position succeeded in avoiding misfortune, he could hardly be expected to escape mistakes. An Irishman by birth, a Roman Catholic by parentage, passionately attached to his race, and devoutly loyal to his religion, he was from the very outset of his career remarkable for the courageous spirit of independence with which he formed and maintained his opinions, no matter whether the subject on which he adventured them was political, historical, or social. A stanza selected from one of his Canadian ballads illustrates this phase of his character, and supplies a key-note to his conduct :

> " Let fortune frown and foes increase,
> And life's long battle know no peace,
> Give me to wear upon my breast
> The object of my early quest,
> Undimm'd, unbroken, and unchang'd,
> The talisman I sought and gain'd,
>   The jewel, Independence !"

Neither was it a mere poetical profession of faith. Mr. McGee's history very clearly shows that he had reason for his rhyme. In the very dew of his youth he maintained his political principles against such an opponent as the great O'Connell, and later still he wore his " Jewel Independence" in the presence of the late Dr. Hughes, the distinguished Archbishop of New York. It is probable that neither of those eminent men viewed with complacency what must have appeared like presumption on the part of their youthful antagonist; but it is pleasant to believe, as we have some reason to believe, that with manly generosity, they did not fail to express their respect for Mr. McGee's abilities, their appreciation of his sincerity, and their desire for his success in life.

The independence which Mr. McGee valued and apostrophized was not the independence which he found in the United States. His second sojourn in that country thoroughly disenchanted him. His early admiration paled before his later experience. The homœopathic principle appears to be susceptible of political as well as physical application, for a taste of democratic institutions cured Mr. McGee of any tendency to democracy. Neither was social life in America more attractive than political life. Both were an offence, and one was an abomination. But the double discovery was made only after a painful and protracted effort not to see it, for it was with great reluctance that his vigorous mind and tenacious will yielded at length to such unwelcome convictions. It would be interesting to read Mr. McGee's own account of his rise and progress towards higher moral and physical latitudes, for every inch of his course might point a moral, every stage of his journey adorn a tale. They only who know with what fanatic faith the human mind will cling even to a cheat, can appreciate the wrench which follows the discovery of the cheat. No man can deliberately break his idol without some sorrowful remembrance of the thing he once thought divine. The testimony of Mr. McGee might enable us to compare the attractions of his fancy with the fallacies of his experience,—the dream-land which his imagination painted and the real land which his eyes saw.

In this interval of conflict, while fighting against himself, and by wager of battle as it were, testing the strength and quality of his principles and opinions, new light, and with it new views, from an unlooked-for quarter, seemed to cross his path. In the midst of literary work in New York he made the acquaintance of many friends.

in Canada. Having formed his own opinions of the people whom he had met, it was natural enough he should wish to see the country where they dwelt. Thus it was that Mr. McGee, during one summer vacation, taking a holiday after the manner of an editor, found himself writing letters to his paper from the shores of Lake Huron, at another from the solitudes of the Ottawa, and at a third from the scenic Provinces of New Brunswick and Nova Scotia. The Provincial attractions were too much for him. He heard in the Provinces what he did not hear in the States, honest opinions openly expressed. He found in the Provinces what he failed to find in the States, a tangible security for freedom. The promise of liberty was no spurious or counterfeit debenture. It was impressed with the stamp of law and endorsed with the sign manual of authority. Whatever may have been the form of the fascination, we find that in the early part of the year 1857, after, as we have the right to suppose, a careful comparison of the two states of society, the American and the Canadian, Mr. McGee transferred, as he has somewhere said, " his household goods to the valley of the St. Lawrence," selecting the City of Montreal as the place of his abode. We may here add that the City of Montreal lost no time in returning the compliment, for on the first opportunity that city elected him as one of its representatives in Parliament, and a little later his friends and neighbors presented him with an exceedingly well-appointed homestead in one of its most eligible localities. It was a hearty Irish mode of making him welcome. Mr. McGee very modestly sought only to be a citizen of the country ; his friends determined that he should be a freeman. No doubt the gift represented a great honor of no uncertain value to the object of it. But apart from such considerations, the shape which the testimonial took, soothed and flattered Irish sentiment. If there be one form of property dearer than another to the offspring of Erin, it is that of a holding ; and no matter whether it be a park or a potato patch, it is equally precious if it promotes the possessor to the condition of an estated gentleman or a landed proprietor.

The old vocation was revived in Mr. McGee's new Home. To write, to print, to publish are with him not only habits of life, but they seem to be modes of enjoyment.

"The long, long weary day
Would pass in grief away,"

at least to him, if it uttered no speech from his pen, or received no thought from his brain. The time which elapsed between his arrival at Montreal, and the isssue of the first number of his newspaper, the " New Era," was brief enough ; but it was nevertheless of sufficient length to enable Mr. McGee to sketch through its columns a policy which harmonized with the name of his paper. He earnestly advocated, and has continued to advocate, ever since that time, an early union of all the Colonies of British North America. In doing so, we may observe in passing, he initiated a phrase as descriptive of his object, which has since become familiar alike from use and criticism, for the proposed confederacy was in his mind and writings associated with the idea of a " new nationality."

At the general election in 1858, Mr. McGee's public career in Canada commenced. He was returned to Parliament as one of the three representatives of Montreal. Whether from hereditary habit, a playful disposition, or serious thought, we know not, but on his arrival in the Province, he lost no time in declaring himself in true Hibernian style to be " against the government." And against the government he undoubtedly was during the four years of the continuance of irritating and acrimonious sixth Parliament. Much of course was expected of him. He had a certain repute as a politician, though he was more distinctly known as a forcible writer, and a fluent speaker. Still his earlier Parliamentary efforts were, we think, followed by disappointment to those who had thought him to be capable of better and wiser things. It was observed that the subject of our sketch was an adroit master of satire, and the most active of partizan sharpshooters. Many severe, some ridiculous, and not a few savage things were said by him. Thus from his affluent treasury of caustic and bitter irony he contributed not a little to the personal and Parliamentary embarrasments of those times. Many of the speeches of that period we would rather forget than remember. Some were not complimentary to the body to which they were addressed, and some of them were not creditable to the persons by whom they were delivered. It is true that such speeches secured crowded galleries, for they were sure to be either breezy or ticklish, gusty with rage, or grinning with jests. They were therefore the raw materials out of which mirth is manufactured, and consequently they provoked irrepressible laughter. Of course they were little calculated to elicit truth, or promote order, or attract respect to the speakers. Indeed men who were inclined to despondency affected little reserve in saying that Parliamentary government was in their opinion a failure. During his early career, Mr. McGee appeared chiefly to occupy himself in saying unpleasant and severe things. This occupation was apt to include the habit of making personal allusions the reverse of agreeable, and, as a matter of course, creating personal enmities the reverse of desirable. In truth, Mr. McGee's speeches at that time were garnished with so many merry jests, and sometimes overlaid with so much rancorous levity, that their more valuable parts were hidden from ordinary eyes, and inappreciable to ordinary minds. The cookery was too generous, the condiments were too spicy. The sauce bore to the substance about the same proportional inequality which Falstaff's "sack" did to his bread; and this deficiency of solidity was attributed by many people to an absence of intellectual property, rather than to an error of conventional taste. Hence arose a disposition on the part of some to underrate Mr. McGee's mental strength, and hence, too, the observation, which, however, was more remarkable for glibness than accuracy, that "Mr. McGee speaks better than he reasons." Certainly the Parliamentary skirmishes of that period, though difficult to defend, were delightful to witness. Human drollery made up in some sort for human naughtiness. There were, for example, two members of that house of great ability, but very dissimilar habits of thought. They sat not far from one another, for if at that day they were not exactly "friends in council," they usually voted together. One was the present Attorney General West, the unrivalled chief of Parliamentary debate ; and the other, the present learned member for Brome, the intellectual detective of suspected fallacies. Breadth and subtlety, reason and casuistry, extensive observation and minute knowledge, marked then as now the peculiar characters of their modes of thought. No matter, however, whether the range of their reasoning was broad or deep, horizontal or vertical, circular or lateral, profound or peculiar, it was commonly acknowledged by the subject of our sketch in a cheerful Irish way, amusing enough to the spectator, but probably not as agreeable to those who looked for grave reflections on grave thoughts. The truth is, that Mr. McGee always seemed to be, in spite of himself, either mischievous or playful; and regardless alike of the place or the occasion, he appeared to be seized with an irresistible impulse to scatter about him an uncomfortable kind of melo-dramatic spray which occasionally drifted and thickened into a rain of searching, infectious, comic banter, which, as a matter of course, amidst roars of laughter, would drown reason, logic and speech in a flood of exuberant fun. Such efforts, however, did not always succeed. Indeed, more clever than praiseworthy, they scarcely deserved success, for people do not always admire what they laugh at. Reaction follows every kind of excess. Members began to talk of decorum of debate, and the necessity of recalling the House to a state of order. None better than Mr. McGee knew that he could, if occasion needed, be grave as well as gay, wise as well as witty, serious as well as jocose. He knew that he could lead thought as well as provoke mirth. He knew that at the fitting time he could make for himself a name, and for his adopted country a place, which would attract respect and honor in both hemispheres.

Having fairly looked his work in the face, Mr. McGee would, as we might reasonably conjecture, cast about him for fitting co-operators. This portion of his public life seems to have been beset with perplexing peculiarities. With an upper-crust of paradox there must, we may suppose, have been an under-current of con-tradiction. As a party man, Mr. McGee chose his side, but in the presence of his declared principles and published opinions it is difficult to understand by what laws his choice was determined. On his arrival in Canada, he had, for reasons which he deemed to be sufficient, declared himself to be "against the Government." Nor can it be denied that for the space of six years he proved the sincerity of his declaration. On the 20th May, 1862, the fortress which he had so persistently battered, fell, for the Cartier-Macdonald administration, which he had opposed and denounced, having been defeated on the motion for reading the Militia Bill the second time, was constrained to resign. In the Sandfield Macdonald-Sicotte administration, which succeeded to power, the subject of our sketch was offered and accepted the office of President of the Council.

B

On the 8th of May following, on a question of want of confidence, the last mentioned administration found itself to be in a minority of five. Four days afterwards Parliament was prorogued with a view to its immediate dissolution. After the prorogation, Mr. Sandfield Macdonald, the leader of the Government, undertook the responsibility of directing what was equivalent to the very hazardous military manœuvre of changing his front in the presence of an active and sagacious enemy. No doubt he was obliged to strengthen his position, and under any circumstances his mode of doing so would be subject to criticism. He reconstructed his government, and the operation included, amongst other changes, not only the sending of his Irish forces to the rear, but of reducing them to the ranks, with the option, as it was amusingly made to appear, of being mustered out of the service. The transaction is of recent occurrence, and need not be dwelt upon. The surprise which it occasioned remains ; for no very specific reasons have been given, so far as we are aware, for the course which was then pursued. That it was not taken upon the advice of the subject of our sketch, we have the best reason for thinking ; for Mr. McGee took the earliest opportunity of showing, in the general election which followed, that he would not play pawn to Mr. Sandfield Macdonald's king. Rather than do so he crossed over to the enemy. The amenities of political elections is a work yet to be written ; when it is written, the election for Montreal, in 1863, might, we incline to think, furnish some instructive as well as amusing passages. In the ession which immediately followed, Mr. McGee, on three different. occasions, and with evident and unalloyed satisfaction, recorded his vote of want of confidence in the re-constructed administration of his former chief. Thus had he fairly crossed the houses He not only, and with a will, voted with the party which he had theretofore opposed, but on the late Sir E. P. Taché, in the month of March following, being called upon to form an administration, and a strong party administration too, he accepted the office of Minister of Agriculture, which he still continues to fill. People may be inclined to think, and not without some reason, that the subject of our sketch was moved in the course which he took, more by pique than by principle, and that a personal slight provoked his political defection. Without staying to discuss a question on which we are not informed, we may, perhaps, be permitted to ask another, which to us, at least, appears to be still more perplexing. What were the circumstances which in the first instance separated Mr. McGee from the party of which he is now a conspicuous member? Were it not ill-mannered to pry, we might, perchance, amuse ourselves by indulging in some idle speculations, and supplement them by making some curious enquiries. If there was one question more than another with which Mr. McGee had identified his name, that question was the union of all the Provinces, and as connected with, and inseparable from it, the questions of National Defence, of the Inter-Colonial Railway, and of Free Inter-Colonial Trade. Happily these questions are not now the property of a party. They belong to the whole of British America, for they have been accepted by the great majority of its inhabitants, as well as by the government and the people of England. Still it should not be forgotten, that these great questions were parts of the cherished policy of the administration which Mr. McGee opposed. The law which regulates political relationships is not easily adjusted, for it is not unfrequently embarrassed with vexatious personal entanglements. In the instance before us, though we may see the affront which impelled, and suspect the causes which attracted him towards his present alliance, we do not see, nor are we required to see, why he served a seven year's apprenticeship to a a party whose policy, in many important particulars, was not only different from, but opposed to his own.

Passing from Mr. McGee's history as a party-man, to his opinions as a public one, we seem to emerge from a bewildering labyrinth of ill-lighted passages, into a succession of *salons* radiant with sunshine. We rise from what may be compared with the unseemly brawls of a parish vestry to the ennobling deliberations of a National Parliament. The vision of the "new era," which Mr. McGee, in his Montreal paper, foreshadowed in 1857, seems to have grown into shape and consistency. In an address delivered at the Temperance Hall, Halifax, in July, 1863, he thus sketches, and with a bold hand, the boundaries of British America, the Northern Empire of the future:

"A single glance at the physical geography of the whole of British America will show that it forms, quite as much in structure as in size, one of the most valuable sections of the globe. Along this eastern coast the Almighty pours the broad Gulf stream, nursed within the tropics, to temper the rigors of our air, to irrigate our 'deep sea pastures,' to combat and subdue the powerful Polar stream which would otherwise, in a single night, fill all our gulfs and harbors with a barrier of perpetual ice. Far towards the west, beyond the wonderful lakes, which excite the admiration of every traveller, the winds that lift the water-bearing clouds from the Gulf of Cortez, and waft them northward, are met by counter-currents which capsize them just where they are essential,—beyond Lake Superior, on both slopes of the Rocky Mountains. These are the limits of that climate which has been so much misrepresented, a climate which rejects every pestilence, which breeds no malaria, a climate under which the oldest stationary population—the French Canadian—have multiplied without the infusion of new blood from France or elsewhere, from a stock of 60,000 in 1760 to a people of 880,000 in 1860. I need not, however, have gone so far for an illustration of the fostering effects of our climate on the European race, when I look on the sons and daughters of this peninsula—natives of the soil for two, three, and four generations—when I see the lithe and manly forms on all sides, around and before me, when I see especially who they are that adorn that gallery (alluding to the ladies), the argument is over, the case is closed. If we descend from the climate to the soil, we find it sown by nature with these precious forests fitted to erect cities, to build fleets and to warm the hearts of many generations. We have the isothern of wheat on the Red River, on the Ottawa, and on the St. John; root crops everywhere; coal in Cape Breton and on the Saskatchewan; iron with us from the St. Maurice to the Trent; in Canada the corper-bearing rocks at frequent intervals from Huron to Gaspé; gold in Columbia and Nova Scotia; salt again, and hides in the Red River region; fisheries inland and seaward unequalled. Such is a rough sketch, a rapid enumeration of the resources of this land of our children's inheritance. Now what needs it this country,—with a lake and river and seaward system sufficient to accommodate all its own, and all its neighbor's commerce,—what needs such a country for its future? It needs a population sufficient in number, in spirit, and in capacity to become its masters; and this population need, as all civilized men need, religious and civil liberty, unity, authority, free intercourse, commerce, security and law."

Again, in the same paper, Mr. McGee exhibits the materials whereof the new nationality shall be composed:

"I endeavor to contemplate it in the light of a future, possible, probable, and I hope to live to be able to to say positive, British American Nationality. For I repeat, in the terms of the questions I asked at first, what do we need to construct such a nationality. Territory, resources by sea and land, civil and religious freedom, these we have already. Four millions we already are: four millions culled from the races that, for a thousand years, have led the van of Christendom. When the sceptre of Christian civilization trembled in the enervate grasp of the Greek of the Lower Empire, then the Western tribes of Europe, fiery, hirsute, clamorous, but kindly, snatched at the falling prize, and placed themselves at the head of human affairs. We are the children of these fire-tried kingdom founders, of these ocean-discoverers of Western Europe. Analyse our aggregate population: we have more Saxons than Alfred had when he founded the English realm. We have more Celts than Brien had when he put his heel on the neck of Odin. We have more Normans than William had when he marshalled his invading host along the strand of Falaise. We have the laws of St. Edward and St. Louis, Magna Charta and the Roman Code. We speak the speeches of Shakespeare and Bossuet. We copy the constitution which Burke and Somers and Sidney and Sir Thomas Moore lived, or died, to secure or save. Out of these august elements, in the name of the future generations who shall inhabit all the vast regions we now call ours, I invoke the fortunate genius of an United British America, to solemnize law with the moral sanction of Religion, and to crown the fair pillar of our freedom with its only appropriate capital, lawful authority, so that hand in hand we and our descendants may advance steadily to the accomplishment of a common destiny."

And at St. John, New Brunswick, in the following month of the same year, Mr. McGee says : " There are before the public men of British America, at this moment, but two courses ; either to drift with the tide of democracy, or to seize the golden moment and fix for ever the monarchical character of our institutions !" " I invite," he continues, " every fellow colonist who agrees with me to unite our efforts that we may give our Province the aspect of an Empire in order to exercise the influence abroad and at home to create a State, and to originate a history which the world will not willingly let die !"

In another part of the same paper, Mr. McGee very solemnly says :

" This being my general view of my own duty—my sincere slow-formed conviction of what a British American policy should be—I look forward to the time when these Provinces, once united, and increasing at an accelerated ratio, may become a Principality worthy of the acceptance of one of the Sons of that Sovereign whose reign inaugurated the firm foundation of our Colonial liberties. If I am right, the Railroad will give us union—union will give us nationality—and nationality, a Prince of the blood of our ancient Kings. These speculations on the future may be thought premature and fanciful. But what is premature in America? Propose a project which has life in it, and while still you speculate, it grows. If that way towards greatness, which I have ventured to point out to our scattered communities be practicable, I have no fear that it will not be taken, even in my time. If it be not practicable, well, then, at least, I shall have this consolation, that I have invited the intelligence of these Provinces to rise above partizan contests and personal warfare to the consideration of great principles, healthful and ennobling in their discussion to the minds of men."

On the same subject, we find in a speech delivered at an earlier day in the Legislative Assembly, the following passage, in which Mr. McGee eloquently groups in one view the main points of his magnificent picture :

" I conclude, Sir, as I began, by entreating the house to believe that I have spoken without respect of persons, and with a sole single desire for the increase, prosperity, freedom and honor of this incipient Northern Nation. I call it a Northern Nation —for such it must become, if all of us do our duty to the last. Men do not talk on this continent of changes wrought by centuries, but of the events of years. Men do not vegetate in this age, as they did formerly in one spot—occupying one portion.

Thought outruns the steam car, and hope outflies the telegraph. We live more in ten years in this era than the Patriarch did in a thousand. The Patriarch might outlive the palm tree which was planted to commemorate his birth, and yet not see so many wonders·as we have witnessed since the constitution we are now discussing was formed. What marvels have not been wrought in Europe and America from 1840 to 1860? And who can say the world, or our own portion of it more particularly, is incapable of maintaining to the end of the century the ratio of the past progress? I for one cannot presume to say so. I look to the future of my adopted country with hope, though not without anxiety. I see in the not remote distance, one great nationality, bound, like the shield of Achilles, by the blue rim of Ocean. I see it quartered into many communities, each disposing of its internal affairs, but all bound together by free institutions, free intercourse, and free commerce. I see within the round of that shield the peaks of the Western Mountains and the crests of the Eastern waves, the winding Assiniboine, the five-fold lakes, the St. Lawrence, the Ottawa, the Saguenay, the St. John, and the basin of Minas. By all these flowing waters in all the valleys they fertilize, in all the cities they visit in their courses, I see a generation of industrious, contented, moral men, free in name and in fact—men capable of maintaining, in peace and in war, a constitution worthy of such a country!"

There are, moreover, throughout the volume of speeches and addresses on "British American Union," passages which appear to be as reverent in their character, as they are eloquent in their language. We deeply regret that our space, and the plan of our work make it impossible for us to lighten this sketch with extensive extracts from Mr. McGee's writings. The manner, for example, in which the political and social systems of the United States re-act upon one another is frequently pointed out with graphic power. He might have, though we do not know that he has, warned his readers that liberty in America may become, for there is great danger of her becoming, a suicide ; and expire wretchedly from some act of unpremeditated violence ; for authority, as it has been truly said, is as necessary to the preservation of liberty as judges are to the administration of law. No violence therefore is done either to sentiment or experience in asserting, that they are most vigilant for freedom, who are most conservative of authority. After this manner Mr. McGee speaks, in closing his speech on the motion for an address to Her Majesty in favor of Confederation :

"We need in these Provinces, and we can bear a large infusion of authority. I am not at all afraid this constitution errs on the side of too great conservatism· If it be found too conservative now, the downward tendency in political ideas which characterizes this democratic age is a sufficient guarantee for amendment. Its conservatism is the principle on which this instrument is strong, and worthy of the support of every colonist, and through which it will secure the warm approbation of the Imperial authorities. We have here no traditions and ancient venerable institutions—here, there are no aristocratic elements hallowed by time or bright deeds—here, every man is the first settler of the land, or removed from the first settler one or two generations at the farthest—here, we have no architectural monuments calling up old associations—here, we have none of those old popular legends and stories which in other countries have exercised a powerful share in the Government—here, every man is the son of his own works. (Hear, hear!) We have none of those influences about us which elsewhere have their effect upon Government, just as much as the invisible atmosphere itself tends to influence life, and animal and vegetable existence. This is a new land—a land of young pretensions, because it is new—because classes and systems have not had time to grow here naturally. We have no aristocracy, but of virtue and talent—which is the best aristocracy, and is the old and true meaning of the term. (Hear, hear!) There is a class of men rising in these colonies superior in many respects to others with whom they might be compared. What I should like to see is—that fair representatives of the Canadian and Acadian aristocracy should be sent to the foot of the Throne with that scheme, to obtain for it the Royal sanction—a scheme not suggested by others or imposed upon us—but one, the work of ourselves, the creation of our own intellect, and of our own free, unbiassed, untrammelled will. I should like to see our best men go there, and endeavor to have this measure carried through the Imperial Parliament—going into Her Majesty's presence, and by their manner, if not actually by their speech, saying—"During Your Majesty's reign we have had Responsible Government conceded to us; we have administered it for nearly a quarter of a century, during which we have under it doubled our population, and more than quadrupled our trade. The small colonies which your ancestors could hardly see on the map, have grown into great communities. A great danger has arisen in our near neighborhood; over our homes a cloud hangs dark and heavy. We do not know when it may burst. With our strength we are not able to combat against the storm, but what we can do, we will do cheerfully and loyally. We want time to grow; we want more people to fill our country—more industrious families of men to develope our resources; we want to increase our prosperity; we want more extended trade and commerce; we want more land tilled —more men established through our wastes and wildernesses; we, of the British North American Provinces, want to be joined together, that if danger comes, we may support each other in the day of trial. We come to Your Majesty, who has given us liberty, to give us unity—that we may preserve and perpetuate our freedom; and whatsoever charter, in the wisdom of your Majesty and of your Parliament you give us, we shall loyally obey and observe, as long as it is the pleasure of your Majesty, and your successors, to maintain the connection between Great Britain and these Colonies."

An opponent of every kind of sectionalism, Mr. McGee is accustomed to say that he neither knows nor wishes to know where the boundary is which divides Upper from Lower Canada. To him the whole is Canada. Rather than occupy himself in discovering boundaries, he would work hard to remove the pickets which separate the British Provinces from one another, that he might strengthen the barriers which protect them from the American States. He would weld them together by such bonds as love forges when he desires to fuse indissoluble ties. Therefore it is that he advocates a policy of conciliation, a policy of forbearance, a policy of defence, a policy of commerce, a policy of intercourse and intimacy, where men's thoughts should be charitable and their lives generous. He professes a statesman's anxiety not to re-enact in Canada the curses which have afflicted Ireland. With this purpose in view, it is his aim to discourage all societies whose object is politically to separate men from one another, to cast them into antagonist associations, or sort them into many-colored coteries, to breed suspicion and create enmity. He believes that there may be unity in plurality, and that the United Provinces like the United Kingdom, though made up of several races, may be tempered and welded into a State, one and indivisible.

Mr. McGee is not only a statesman and an orator—he is also, as most people are aware, a lecturer of no ordinary gifts, and an author of no ordinary ability. His range of subjects in the former character is perplexingly extensive, and suggests the notion that the nooks and crannies of his brain must be as thickly peopled with thoughts as are the tenements of the fifth and sixth wards of New York, with his ill-treated and closely-packed countrymen. To many of us it is a matter of regret that we know nothing more of those lectures than their names.* With respect to Mr. McGee's works, we shall in this place content ourselves with a list of their titles only.†

Mr. McGee left Ireland for the second time in 1848. He returned to Ireland for the second time in 1865. Between that coming and that going, his personal history had been stamped with

---

*The subjects include papers on Columbus, Shakespeare, Milton, Burke, Grattan, Burns, Moore, The Reformation, The Jesuits, The English Revolution of 1688, The growth and power of the Middle Classes in England, The Moral of the Four Revolutions, The Irish Brigade in the service of France, The American Revolution, The Spirit of Irish History, Will and Skill.

† O'Connell and his Friends, 1 vol., Boston, 1844; The Irish Writers of the Seventeenth Century, 1 vol., Dublin, 1856; Life of McMurrough, 1 vol., Dublin, 1847; Memoir of Duffy, Pamphlet, Dublin, 1849; Historical Sketches of Irish Settlers in America. 1 vol., Boston, 1850; History of the Reformation in Ireland, 1 vol., Boston, 1852; Catholic History of North America, 1 vol., Boston, 1852; Life of Bishop Maginn, 1 vol., New York, 1856; Canadian Ballads, Montreal, 1 vol., New York, 1858; Popular History of Ireland, 2 vols., New York, 1862; Notes on Federal Governments, past and present, Pamphlet, Montreal, 1864; Speeches on British American Union, London, 1865.

strange vicissitudes, and his political opinions had undergone serious changes. He left Ireland because failure had waited upon folly ; but then we can imagine he was oblivious to every recollection but the self-evident one of failure. He returned, too, not only because wisdom had been crowned with success, but because he could think of his previous failure, if not with complacency, at least without either regret or shame. On both occasions he was equally sincere, and perhaps even when he was most wrong he was most in earnest. It was not, however, as a private, much less as an obscure individual, that he was required to re-visit his native land. He did so by command of the Queen's representative, as a Commissioner from Canada. He did so, furthermore, as a member of the Executive Council for the purpose of joining his colleagues in conference with the representatives of Her Majesty's Government. When last in Ireland he took the opportunity of publicly explaining to his countrymen the true position, actual and comparative, of the Irish race in America. The force and originality of the statements and opinions contained in his eloquent and celebrated Wexford speech, attracted unusual attention. The press and public men of Great Britain and Ireland had much to say of the speaker and his speech ; and no wonder, for recent events have taught them, and us, that there was in what he said prophetic, as well as philosophic, truth.

In his personal appearance, Mr. McGee is what our portrait represents him to be. The photographer and the sunbeam seem to have understood one another admirably, when they turned Mr. McGee upside down in the camera; for he has come out of the trial with incomparable exactness. The shadows of the outward man have been caught with felicitous accuracy. The intellectual man, if reproduced at all, must be reproduced by resorting to a process analogous to that which has been observed by the artist with respect to the physical man. Light from without enables us to see what Mr McGee is naturally. Light from within must enable us to see what he is intellectually. The mirror work of his mind is reflected in his words, and they who would examine its brightness, must do so in the pages of his writings.

The great gifts of genius which Divine Providence occasionally bestows, are, we believe, conferred as special trusts, for special uses.

The subject of our sketch may have been, perchance he was, a chosen trustee of special gifts. He works as if, within the folds of the scheme which he has set himself to accomplish, there were many purposes of wisdom and charity. Directly, he desires by means of confederation to bring about the intimate union of several Provinces. Indirectly, he desires by a policy of conciliation, to bring about the fusion of various races, and thus to supplement the law which shall create a new nation, with a policy which shall create a new nationality.

Nor are such plans purposeless, or such hopes chimerical. The races which inhabit British America represent peoples whose countries are made up of various tribes and different languages. The laws of moral like those of physical gravitation have not ceased to operate. The smaller bodies will be attracted, and eventually absorbed by the larger ones. What the United Kingdom is, the United Provinces will become. The question is one of time, and not of legislation. But the process of transition to be accomplished wisely, must be accomplished without violence and especially without wrong. The pursuit of such a purpose is worthy of a Christian statesman, and a philosophic patriot. If Mr. McGee, as one of many, shall succeed in giving shape and consistency to the vision of "a fraternal era," which he has foreshadowed, which the late Sir E. P. Taché foresaw, and which the most experienced of our own statesmen are striving to bring about, many good men will envy, and all good men will praise him. If he fail, though there should be no such word as failure, his great disappointment will at all events be solaced with

> "A peace above all other dignities,
> A still and quiet conscience."

*In the possession of a "still and quiet conscience" the gifted orator and the brave patriot has in this world won "dignities" and in the world to come, where "good deeds are had in remembrance," we doubt not he has found peace. It is hard to dwell on the ruthless

---

* This sketch was thus far written and published in the life time of Mr. McGee. We have not thought fit to change what was written, but now the past must be substituted for the present tense, for alas! the subject belongs to their histories who have passed away.

character of the act which has given to eternity one, with reverence be it said, whose life was so valuable to time. It is idle, and perchance wrong, to challenge His decrees without whom even a sparrow falls not; and yet all intelligence is at fault, all reasoning vain as we view his majestic wreck, who was so great and so greatly feared; so great and so greatly loved—but alas! "the golden bowl is broken."

> "Ay! broken by a fiendish hand,
> Impell'd by felon thought;
> Seek not, oh! man, to understand
> Why such a wreck was wrought.

Why in the meridian of his age, in the zenith of his usefulness; scarcely beyond the morning of his fame, and only in the dawn of his honors, should his bright career have been brought to such a cruel end; are questions as vain to ask, as impossible to answer. The blood-stained facts are related by different persons in nearly the same words, and in similar phrases telegraphed to different parts of the world. Thus the tidings read.

" OTTAWA, April 7th, 3.00 a.m.

" Mr. McGee left the House of Commons before two o'clock, the moon making it nearly as light as day. He was accompanied by Mr. McFarlane, also a member of the House. They separated at the corner of the street for their respective lodgings. When they said " good night" Mr. McGee was not more than one hundred yards from his hotel. He was smoking a cigar and carried his walking stick under his left arm. His right hand was occupied in finding the latch key wherewith it was his practice to pass through the private door to his rooms. It is conjectured that as he stooped to place the key in the door, an assassin from some place of convenient concealment, shot him from behind, placing the muzzle of the pistol close to his head. The ball came out of his mouth destroying his front teeth and burying itself in the framework of the door, and from the nature of the wound, causing instant death." The pestilent breath of the miscreant must momentarily at least have mingled with his victim's, for they were in such close proximity as to cause the hair of the latter to be singed and the flesh scorched by the flash of the shot. Thus was " the golden bowl.

broken," and thus were scattered the garnered treasures of his seething brain; scattered, too, when he was actively coining thoughts of sterling value to the country of his adoption as well as the country of his birth.

It is difficult for those who knew him well, to hold a steady pen or write with calm coherency of his great intellectual powers, and yet it is desirable not to overlook a personal fact, his triumphant, moral mastery of himself. We may speak now without either shame or shock, of the earnest character of his efforts to bring about an exact correspondence between the tastes that injured him, and the teachings that benefited others. It was no easy trial for one of his exuberant mirth, his social predilections and his convival habits, to lay aside the evil which had become associated with such experiences, and yet retain the experiences apart from the evil; to preserve the relish for the friendship, and yet put from him the wine which he had esteemed as the almost inseparable associate of such friendship: to put away from him what theologians would term "his besetting sin," and yet retain the grace and brightness of character from which it sprang. Mr. McGee did so, and as we are informed, without resorting to any stimulating test or public pledge, but by bending his strong will to the vow which he had registered in the cloister of his soul, and which he had presented to the supreme source of strength. "I have made my resolve," said he to his attending physician, who, despairing of his life, recommended him to take some stimulants. "I have made my resolve, and not to save life itself will I break through it." He lived long enough to convince the most incredulous that he had won this great victory over himself, and that from thenceforward there was little fear of his mental strength being impaired by moral weakness. When he was so unconsciously drawing near the close of his life, it is something worthy of record that the follies and stains which had disfigured that life, one after another, were overcome and cast out, leaving him at length "renewed, regenerate and disenthralled" by the threefold powers of virtue, temperance, and charity.

To return to our narrative. Many of our readers are aware that the former portion of this sketch was written two years ago when Mr. McGee was in Europe. He had made his celebrated Wexford speech, and had attracted towards himself thereby no small amount of attention on the part of the public men of England, and, we may add, no small amount of aversion on the part of the fiendish fraternity, whose machinations were on that occasion so eloquently described and so fearlessly exposed. Incidentally, and in his private capacity, he was encouraged to represent his views on the policy which English statesmen should observe in the government of Ireland; and it is probable that such representations may have given rise to the opinion which the Earl of Mayo lately expressed in the House of Commons, that Mr. McGee was the foremost defender of British institutions in the Queen's dominions. "To his countrymen, if we recollect aright, he said on that occasion—there ought to be, no separation of the Kingdoms of England and Ireland. Each country would suffer from the loss of the other, and even liberty in Europe would be shipwrecked if those islands were divided by a hostile sea. To Englishmen, he said, try kindness and generosity in your legislation for Ireland. Treat Ireland as you have treated Scotland—consider her feelings, and respect her prejudices—study her history, and concede her rights—try equal justice to all—practice the golden rule and "do as you would be done by." Then will Irishmen in Ireland resemble Irishmen in Canada, when the Celt is not envious of the Saxon, and the Saxon is not supercilious to the Celt. Whether or not Mr. McGee's representations produced any effect on the minds of those to whom they were addressed, we have no means of knowing; still, it is noteworthy that the policy in regard to Ireland which seems to find most favour at the present time very much resembles the policy, based on equal rights and equal respects for all origins, all races, and all creeds which he is understood to have submitted, when the opportunity was afforded him of making a representation of his views, to influential statesmen at home.

Though not a delegate Mr. McGee as a member of the Executive Council of Canada, was in a position to render his colleagues great assistance when they were engaged in carrying the act of confederation through the Imperial Parliament. The object which that act brought about was an object of absorbing interest to Mr. McGee, and without detracting from the wisdom or sagacity of any other statesman we may perhaps say that his writings did much towards.

making the project popular in the minds, while his speeches made it pleasant to the hearts of men. Neither has the question found since then a more eloquent, a more consistent or a more enthusiastic advocate than the subject of this sketch; for it had become not only the principle aim of his existence but the very passion of his life. With his mind thus occupied Mr. McGee was appointed a Commissioner from Canada to the Paris Exposition, yet even there amidst the bewildering attractions of social and intellectual life, amidst the representatives of every tongue and tribe from " China to Peru," and encompassed with the surroundings " in number without number,—numberless," of ancient and modern art; yet even there, with such drawbacks and distractions, his best thoughts turned lovingly to that new Dominion whose foundation his industry had helped to lay, and whose superstructure his genius was assisting to build. His mind though attracted by culture nevertheless turned from the charms of Paris and the loveliness of France, from its pleasant homesteads and its profitable vineyards, from its intellectual and its heroic history to the seat of another sovereignty and the site of another empire—an empire.

> " Whose flanks were mighty oceans,
> Whose base the Northern pole."

And there, in the central city of civilization, the emporium of art and the abode of fashion, he gathered his thoughts, and addressed his remarkable letter of the 1st May, 1867, to his constituents at Montreal, and through them to the inhabitants of the New Dominion, wherein he counselled them after what manner they might hope to win a place in the family of states, which few European nations had attained, and which none had surpassed. It was, we have reason to know his intention to have supplemented that letter with another, but for reasons of a political, as well as of a personal kind, he deemed it advisable to postpone its publication.

The arrangements consequent on the formation of the first Privy Council of the New Dominion, did not include a portfolio for Mr. McGee. To the regret of many persons and the surprise of all, he was, at his own generous and spontaneous desire, left out. The history of the transaction has not so far, as we are aware, been made public, but there can be no doubt whatever that Mr. McGee would not allow his personal wishes or his political claims to stand in the way of the harmonious action of the new experiment. His pride might have rebelled, or his poverty might have clamored, but honor and patriotism rebuked the one and silenced the other. He might have said, and probably did say, " don't consider me or my claims, look to the state and its welfare." Thus it chanced that the minister who was most generally known in the Maritime Provinces, and as well known in Ontario and Quebec, as any member of the administration, who had spoken more eloquently, and written more earnestly on the duties and advantages of union and confederation, waived all claims to be considered when that union was officially brought about, and the statesmen who were first called upon to work it, were announced in the official *Gazette*.

No doubt the waiver was a sacrifice of feeling at the shrine of duty, but it is pleasant to know that it was unattended with any sacrifice of friendship. We believe indeed that moved by the generosity of his character, Mr. McGee withdrew his claim to office with such a steady purpose as to draw from Sir John A. Macdonald a remonstrance at the hurried character of the proceeding. By acting as he did, Mr. McGee thought to relieve Sir John of certain embarrassments. Nor was the supposition ill-founded, for it was said that his timely generosity overcame several very disturbing difficulties. Thus was it that the Minister of Justice and the Minister of Militia continued to be fast friends of Mr. McGee and he of them to the last hour of his life.

After the Privy Councillors were sworn in, new elections took place. It occasioned but small surprise to Mr. McGee that the felonious organizations which he had denounced when in England, and which he had sought to expose on his return to Canada, excited every influence they could command to exchange opposition and resistance on their parts for assault and exposure on his. Like the members of such associations he knew something of secret organizations for violent purposes. He was not unacquainted with the mischievous character of the machinery by which such associations were supported and kept in motion. He was not unfamiliar with the oaths, or ignorant of the constitutions of such orders, and being in some sort, acquainted with their pernicious structure and dangerous tendency, he was enabled to speak with emphasis of things as they were and counsel with authority of things as they ought to be. But advice was received with contempt and reproof was met with resistance. The innocent blood so freely shed at Ridgeway provoked neither compassion nor thought. The Satanic league across the southern frontier but too successfully impregnated certain localities in Canada with the sulphur of their sin. Being the largest city of the Dominion, Montreal was supposed to contain the greatest number of Fenian sympathisers, while the especial section which Mr. McGee represented was regarded as the chosen spot of the "Local Head Centre." While it was not possible for Mr. McGee to have exaggerated the evil which such an organization was calculated to bring about, it is possible that he took an extreme view of its local influence, and a mistaken one of the individuals by whom it was sustained and defended. Thus when he somewhat rashly published what he knew, the disclosure fell far short of the public expectation and peradventure of his own belief. He said either too much or too little, and hence his reputation for acuteness acquired no strength from what he then deemed it to be his duty to disclose. The election which followed, though it resulted in a majority in his favor, of two hundred and eighty-four votes, shewed a serious defection in a certain class of his Irish supporters, and gave strength to the belief that the leaven of mischief had not altogether been inopperative. It was a melancholy return of ingratitude, a base recompense to one who beyond all living Irishmen had accomplished most good for his country and his countrymen. But the wave of sedition still flowed from the United States. In a public address at Buffalo, within sight of the shores where many of our youth had without provocation been foully slain, Senator Morrison, of Tennessee, is reported to have said of those Irishmen, who would not enrol themselves in their fiendish enterprise, "the recreant traitors who refuse to join this organization will be handed down to posterity with the names of Benedict Arnold, Judas Iscariot, and D'Arcy McGee." If such words might be spoken in the open, what might not have been determined upon in the secret councils of those who could coolly make covenants for blood? Underlying and concurrent with such allusions were ominous threats against his life, which, in various forms, but pointing to one issue, beset Mr. McGee almost everywhere. He was dogged and watched. His house, at the instance of his friends, was put under the surveillance of the police. He was neither fool-hardy nor insensible of the risk he ran, or of the implacable character of the foes by whom he was surrounded. He had, however, long since settled his account with his conscience and determined irrespective of consequences to do his duty to his Sovereign, to his country and to himself. Nevertheless, as the Honorable Mr. Chauveau beautifully observed, even while he was thus pursuing the paths of charity, loyalty and honor, the shadowed hand of the assassin was upon him, pursuing him with that kind of stealthy craft with which the brute in his instinct hungers for the man.

As his strength permitted Mr. McGee availed himself of several opportunities to inculcate his lessons of mutual .consideration and mutual good will. Under various pretexts the same duties were enforced. We read them, and feel the friendly touch of his generous helping hand in his lecture on the " Mental outfit of the New Dominion." In his speeches at Ottawa on the last anniversary of his patron Saint ; in his sketch of the history of English literature, in his speeches in Parliament, and especially in that last speech made by him just before the debate closed which immediately preceded the hush and silence of his silver tongue. Incidentally the question of the repeal of the Union between Canada and Nova Scotia, became a subject of conversation in the House of Commons, when Mr. McGee, true to his own convictions, and his mission of good will and peace, informed those who favored such a project that time would smooth difficulties and heal discontent, that justice would overcome prejudice, and that the magic of kindness would at length triumph and make converts of all. It is to be regretted that no full report of those last, words was made. Had we possessed fore-knowledge, how keen would have been the hearing ear, how active the untiring pen ! We shall transcribe a fragment, the closing passage of that speech, as it is reported in the *Ottawa Times:*

He had great reliance on the mellowing effects of time to aid the softening and healing influence of the pervading principles of impartial justice, which would happily permeate the whole land, and eventually convert the Honorable member for Lunenburg into the heartiest supporter of Union within these walls, willing and anxious to perpetuate the system which would be found to work so advantageously for his Province, adopting the position of the Honorable member for Guysborough, as that of the true and patriotic statesman. It had been said that

C

the interests of Canada were diametrically opposed to those of Nova Scotia, but he asked which of the parties to the Union' partnership had embarked most in it, or had most to fear from its failure. He asserted that Nova Scotia prejudice would be overcome ere long by the even and high-minded justice with which the Confederation would be administered—a Confederation to whose whole history no stigma could be attached, and whose single aim from the beginning had been to consolidate the extent of British America, with the utmost regard to the powers and privileges of each Province. He did not speak there as a representative of any race, or any Province, but as emphatically a Canadian, ready and bound to recognize the claims of any of his' Canadian fellow subjects from east to west as those of his nearest neighbor who had proposed him at the hustings. (Applause.)

And with such sentiments on his lips, his public life in Canada was brought to a consistent end. A few minutes later, and the assassin's bullet made space enough for his spirit to escape the thrall of the flesh; and alas! by the same act, to make a blank in our Legislature by the destruction its most glorious portion in the " Mental outfit of the New Dominion." Horror and indignation walked through our thoroughfares and grief found congenial articulation in the language of passion. "The fir tree howl'd, for the cedar had fallen." The press groaned with sorrow while on its teeming pages, passages bright with tears, bore eloquent testimony to the merits of the dead. The Government of the Dominion, the Legislatures of the Provinces, and the Corporations of Cities, seemed to vie with one another in the amount of the rewards which should be paid for the discovery of the murderer. In the meanwhile, the pavement where that pool of human blood lay was sacredly enclosed, no foot was allowed to cross it. It was left, some said, to cry to heaven for vengeance; and others said that like the blood of a sacrifice, it was as an offering of peace to the wicked passions of men.

We shall insert what is without doubt a very imperfect report, extracted from a local newspaper, of what followed later in the day.

HOUSE OF COMMONS.

OTTAWA, April 7th, 1868.

The SPEAKER took the chair at ten minutes past three.
The galleries were densely crowded.
Sir JOHN A. MACDONALD rose amidst the breathless silence of the House and manifesting feelings of the most profound emotion, which for some time almost stopped his utterance, said:—Mr. Speaker, it is with pain amounting to anguish that I rise to address you. He who last night, nay this morning, was with

us and of us, whose voice is still ringing in our ears, who charmed us with his marvellous eloquence, elevated us by his large statesmanship, and instructed us by his wisdom and his patriotism, is no more—is foully murdered. If ever a soldier who fell on the field of battle in the front of the fight, deserved well of his country, Thomas D'Arcy McGee deserved well of Canada and its people. The blow which has just fallen is too recent, the shock is too great, for us yet to realize its awful atrocity, or the extent of this most irreparable loss. I feel, Sir, that our sorrow, our genuine and unaffected sorrow, prevents us from giving adequate expression to our feelings just now, but by and by, and at length, this House will have a melancholy pleasure in considering the character and position of my late friend and colleague. To all, the loss is great, to me I may say inexpressibly so; as the loss is not only of a warm political friend, who has acted with me for some years, but of one with whom I enjoyed the intercommunication of his rich and varied mind; the blow has been overwhelming. I feel altogether incapable of addressing myself to the subject just now. Our departed friend was a man of the kindest and most generous impulse, a man whose hand was open to every one, whose heart was made for friendship, and whose enmities were written in water; a man who had no gall, no guile; "in wit a man, in simplicity a child." He might have lived a long and respected life had he chosen the easy path of popularity rather than the stern one of duty. He has lived a short life, respected and beloved, and died a heroic death; a martyr to the cause of his country. How easy it would have been for him, had he chosen, to have sailed along the full tide of popularity with thousands and hundreds' of thousands, without the loss of a single plaudit, but he has been slain, and I fear slain because he preferred the path of duty. I could not help being struck with his language last night, which I will quote from the newspaper report. "He hoped " that the mere temporary or local popularity would not in that house, be made the " test of qualification for public service; that rested simply on popularity, and " he who would risk the right, in hunting for popularity, would soon find that which " he hunted for slip away. Base indeed would he be who could not risk popularity " in a good cause; that of his country." He has gone from us, and it will be long ere we find such a happy mixture of eloquence, wisdom and impulse. (Hear, hear.) His was no artificial or meretricious eloquence, every word of his was as he believed, and every belief of his was in the direction of what was good and true. Well may I say now, on behalf of the Government and of the country, that, if he has fallen, he has fallen in our cause, leaving behind him a grateful recollection which will ever live in the hearts and minds of his countrymen. We must remember too that the blow which has fallen so severely on this House and the country will fall more severely on his widowed partner and his bereaved children. He was too good, too generous to be rich. He hast left us, the government, the people, and the representatives of the people, a sacred legacy, and we would be wanting in our duty to this country and to the feeling which will agitate the country from one end to the other, if we do not accept that legacy as a sacred trust, and look upon his widow and children as a widow and children belonging to the State. (Hear, hear.) I now move that the House adjourn, and that it stand adjourned till Tuesday next, at half past seven.

Mr. McKENZIE said, in rising to second this motion, I find it almost impossible to proceed, but last night we were all charmed by the eloquence of our departed friend, who is now numbered with our honoured dead, and none of us dreamed when we separated last, that we should so very soon be called in this way to record our affection for him who had been thus suddenly cut off. It was my own lot for many years to work in political harmony with him, and it was my lot sometimes to oppose him, but through all the vicissitudes of political warfare we ever found him possess that generous disposition characteristic of the man and his country;

and it will be long as the Hon. Knight at the head of the Government has said before we shall see his like again amongst us. I think there can be no doubt upon the mind of any one who has watched the events of last year in our country, in connection with events in his own distant native land, that he has fallen a victim to the noble and patriotic course which he has pursued in this country ; having been assassinated by one of those who are alike the enemies of our country and of mankind. (Hear, hear.) I cordially sympathise with all that has been uttered by the honourable gentleman at the head of the Government, in making this motion and I have no fear that the generosity of Canadians will fail when it comes to be considered what we owe to his memory, and what we owe to his family. I would gladly, if I could, speak for a few minutes regarding the position he held amongst us, but I cannot do more to-day than simply record my full appreciation of his public character as an orator, a statesman and a patriot, and express the fervent hope that his family thus suddenly bereaved of him who was at once their support and their shield, will not, so far as comforts of this life can be afforded, suffer by his death, and that as the consolation that can be given by those who have been long his companions in public life, by that sentiment of universal sorrow which prevails in every heart, will be brought to the hearts of those more immediately connected with him, his wife and children. This is the first instance we have had in our country of any of our great public men being stricken down by the hand of the assassin, and grief for our loss, and grief for his family are mingled in my mind with a profound feeling of shame and regret that such a thing could, by any possibility, happen in our midst, and I can only hope that the efforts to to made by Government will lead to the discovery that to an alien hand is due the sorrow that now clouds not only this house but the whole community. (Hear, hear.)

Mr. CARTIER—Mr. Speaker, I will state at the outset that my heart is filled with feelings of deepest sorrow. I had the pleasure and delight in common with all the members of this house, to listen last night to the charming eloquence of the representative of the city of Montreal, and no one expected at that moment, that any one of us should be here speaking to-day on such a lamentable evil as that which befell us immediately after the adjournment of the house. I feel deep regret at this moment that I am not gifted with that power of speech, that power of description, that power of eloquence, which distinguished our departed friend. I could make use of such power to bring back before you, sir, and before this house, in proper language the great loss we have suffered, the loss the country has suffered, and the loss mankind has suffered, in the death of Thomas D'Arcy McGee. (Hear, hear.) Our colleague, Mr. McGee, was not an ordinary man; he was, I may say, one of those great, gifted minds, whom it pleases Providence sometimes to set before the world, in order to show to what a height the intellect of man can be exalted by the Almighty. Mr. McGee adopted this land of Canada, as his country, but although this was the land of his adoption he never ceased to love his mother country, his dear old Ireland. In this adopted land of his he did all in his power in order that his countrymen should be rendered as happy as possible, whether their lot was cast in this country, in Ireland, or in any part of the globe where an Irishman had set his foot. Mr. McGee though very young had a great deal of experience. He was connected with political events in Ireland in 1848 and there is not the least doubt that those painful times caused him to give the deepest consideration to those political evils, though he was, as described by my honourable friend the leader of Government, a man of impulse, of genius, and of wisdom, it is very seldom we meet a man on earth having those fine gifts who was so judicious as our late colleague. He was educated as it were for the benefit of his country. He is no longer among us, and I suppose all of my listeners at this moment will say with me that it has not been given to any one of us to have ever listened to so eloquent a public man. Every one of us shares the conviction that such happiness, such delight will never be given hereafter to any one of us during our life time. He has left us. He has left behind him expressions of his feeling of patriotism and an immense amount of evidence, that no Irishman, on earth, loved so much as he did dear Ireland. Mr. Speaker, I cannot but allude at this moment to that foreign organization in the land inhabited by our neighbours. I have not the least doubt that Mr. McGee, by warning the Irishmen of Canada not to join in that detestable organization, rendered the greatest service that an Irishman can render to his country. (Hear, hear.) He acquired for the Irish inhabitants of Canada the inestimable reputation of loyalty and of freedom from any participation in the hateful, detestable feelings and doings of the members of that abominable institution, the Fenian organization. (Hear, hear.) Now that he is no longer amongst us, that he has passed from life to death, it is very likely that his death was the work of an assassin in that organization. It is not for us at this moment to excite feelings of revenge against the perpetrators of such an abominable act, but every one of us knows this, that if Thomas D'Arcy McGee had not taken the patriotic stand which he took before and during the Fenian invasion of this country, he would not be lying a corpse this morning. At all events, sir, every Irishman inhabiting the different Provinces of Canada, when they consider the services Thomas D'Arcy McGee rendered to them in order to induce them not to partake in that Fenian movement in the United States, will lament his death as much as any one of us. Now, Mr. Speaker, I will not allude to his private qualities. I have known him; and we know that of this world's goods he possessed very little. He was a poor man, but I know myself that feelings of of charity swelled his heart. The little he had, he was always willing to share with his poor countrymen. Although he was so gifted, although he soared so high above the ablest man in the land, did he ever show a feeling of vanity, did he ever show, by even a word, that he was more gifted than any one else in the land? No! but he used all his great power and ability modestly, for the good of his native land and his adopted country. I do hope and trust that this great Dominion will not leave helpless his widow and his dear children. He has not fallen, it is true, upon the field of battle; it cannot be said that he met the fate of a military hero; but his end was that of a Parliamentary hero. For two or three years he knew the bad passions which existed among certain classes on the other side of the lines. Again and again he received, through newspapers and other means, warning of the fate which he met last night. Well, did that prevent him from continuing his good work of inducing his countrymen to have nothing to do with that detestable organization? No! he laboured on, and now that he is no longer amongst us, we feel that the Irish inhabitants of the Dominion will appreciate the services he has rendered to them, and that they will mingle their tears with ours for his irreparable loss. (Hear, hear.)

Mr. CHAMBERLIN said: When profound grief, such as now reigns in this House, weighs down men's hearts, few words are best. Yet I am loth that we should depart ere some tribute of respect has been paid, some words of regret uttered, even in this place, in behalf of the fraternity of letters, to which the deceased belonged. It is fit it should be spoken, even though to come from a member of what is held to be the lower branch of the literary craft to which I belong, in which, too, our deceased friend has had a no mean honour to win a distinguished place. (Hear, hear.) His love of letters, and the great diversity of his writings, are well known. Of his diligence in promoting the cause of literature, his endeavours to promote a love of letters amid the young men of Montreal, and of the whole Dominion, it has been my privilege also to know much. He had made himself known in Canada and abroad as a letturer, essayist, historian and poet. Others have spoken in fitting terms of the matchless oratory with which he clothed statesmanlike thought, and of his labours to allay intesti.e strife and promote the highest interests of the country, for which he has lost his life. But the press and literature of Canada must also mourn to-day for their brightest light extinguished; their greatest man prematurely reft from them, as he has been, for his country. (Applause.)

Mr. ANGLIN said : I would be unworthy of my position in the House if I did not take this occasion to join in the expressions of horror and detestation which I know every member of this House, every man worthy of the name of a man, in this Dominion, must feel at the atrocious crime which has been committed. (Hear, hear.) I feel peculiarly embarrassed on this occasion, because it has been assumed, and I fear only too correctly, that this foul assassination has been the work of an organization of Irishmen—not I trust of Irishmen belonging to this Dominion—though I think it will not require much intelligence to determine that any Irishman who has enjoyed the free institutions of this country could not be guilty of such a dastardly act, (hear, hear,) but I cannot help thinking nevertheless, that as wherever Irishmen are—they are all one people—the crime of one will reflect on them all. I think I may speak on behalf of the whole of the Irishmen of this Dominion, I am sure I may on behalf of those of my own province, in expressing our utter destestation of this crime. It is an outrage that will probably have a great effect on the future of this country. None of us can realize its effects yet, the shock is too recent, none of us can, on this occasion, give vent to the feeling which overmasters us. Perhaps after all this is the highest tribute which we can pay to the man who has gone from amongst us. This must be the most telling mode of showing to our countrymen what our feelings are, and that we all agree in stigmatizing a crime of this nature. (Hear, hear.) I go even further than those who have preceded me, and express the hope that the assassin shall be speedily brought to justice. Not that we shall indulge in feelings of vengeance, but that all the means at the command of the Government shall be put forth to point out this assassin wherever he may be concealed; that the death of Mr. McGee may be revenged, and that the supremacy of the law may be maintained. (Hear, hear.) I feel myself, Mr. Speaker, quite incapable of adequately expressing my feelings on this occasion, but I could not allow the opportunity to pass without saying those few words. (Applause.)

Mr. CHAUVEAU said I also must pay my tribute of homage to him who has just fallen the victim of a crime of which we have truly said that it is without precedent in the history of our country. I recall the eloquent speech which he made even last night, in which one would search in vain for a single word, which could wound or irritate in the least degree, the feelings of those to whom he particularly addressed himself. (Hear, hear.) Those who had heard him can bear testimony that the advices and counsels were not given with a spirit of provocation, but on the contrary, they were given in a spirit of conciliation and concord. Those who heard him can truly judge that this spirit animated him last night, in his remarks on the subject of Nova Scotia. They can remember that he terminated his speech in saying that he fervently hoped that the debate would not have any unfavourable results for the country, and would not produce any evils to this province. A like crime has happily no precedent in the history of our country, and were it possible for us to console ourselves for the loss which we have sustained in the death of a friend; of an eminent man—of the prince of orators; we would find that consolation in the glory and relation of his death. That death is the baptism in blood of Confederation, and the sacrifice of him who did so much to bring about that Confederation, is a fact which ought to raise us in our own estimation, and make us judge of the height of our mission. If Mr. McGee had not fallen on the battle-field, his death is none the less glorious, because as the consummation of a grand idea, of a grand principle, that of the Union of the colonies. As the heroes on the field of battle, so the soldiers of grand causes are ever in danger, and great things are never done except at the peril of the lives of those who accomplish them, and nevertheless, his patriotism has made him disdain that danger, and the fear of that danger never caused him to recoil in the struggle which he had undertaken against those whose hand struck him last night. (Hear, hear.) Warnings to him had not been wanting, either publicly—through the press, or in the sinister form of threatening letters; but his great soul disdained these threats, and nothing detained him from the great task which he had undertaken. Truly, if that death 's a glorious one for the country, it is a sensible and terrible loss for his family. Even yesterday he presented a petition in favour of the representatives and the family of a hero, that of Colonel De Salaberry. He told me what he proposed to submit and to ask the House, to come to the aid of the descendants of De Salaberry, and a few hours later he himself fell as a hero and left a family without support, without hope, and without fortune. The name of D'Arcy McGee will live in the History of Canada, and his death will mark the death of Fenianism, for never has cause gained by assassination. No! from Julius Cæsar to the Rienzi, down to Mr. Lincoln, never has a cause succeeded by assassination; and the death of their great men was the signal of the death of the cause of the party under the blows of which they fell, as the death of D'Arcy McGee will be the signal of the death of the party which exercised its vengeance on him. I think that the murder of the Hon. Mr. McGee will have a happy influence upon Canada, inasmuch as it will force that spirit of disloyalty heretofore prevalent to disappear, and inspire a horror of the party which gave it birth; while, at the same time, it will contribute to the glory and the greatness of Canada. As happily has been said, the Hon. Mr. McGee never displayed the least vanity, or prided himself upon his transcendent talent. He was always modest and affable towards all, and never appeared to appreciate his own merit. He also had a generous heart. He was always ready to contribute to every charity or charitable institution. I have often met him in Montreal in ceremonies and public celebrations got up for the purpose of doing good and instilling charity, and he never refused his aid or refused to draw on the eloquent fund of words which sprung from the bottom of his heart in aid of the poor. On these occasions he always seemed to be under the impression that he was only doing what another person would have done, and his good heart was equal to his modesty. The orphans and unfortunates have lost in him a great protector, but he also behind him leaves a widow and some orphans. To-day we must perforce deplore his death. To-morrow, or at another sitting of the House, we will have a duty to fulfil towards his memory and his family (hear, hear), and I am happy to see that the Government has already thought of an act of reparation, an act of justice; and I am sure that so far as the Province of Quebec is concerned, whatever sum the Government proposes, that Province will heartily concur in. The Hon. gentleman, whose speech was delivered in French, seemed to be considerably affected, and was listened to with marked attention.

Mr. E. M. MACDONALD (Lunenburgh, N. S.,) said: Mr. Speaker, I feel utterly unable to express the feelings which at this moment almost overpowers me. How little did I dream when I heard the lamented deceased last night, that it would be the last time this House would listen to him. When I think that that active teeming brain has ceased for ever to animate what is now but his cold clay, I stand aghast. It was my lot to be among those who viewed some political events from a different stand of point from that of the honourable deceased. But whatever difference of opinion there may have been upon political matters, on oue point there can be no difference of opinion on his genial nature, his kindly heart, and the wide charity that animated him. When he departed he left us not his equal behind him. With regard to the heinousness of the monstrous crime that has been committed, I feel unable to express myself, but this I must say that not only the honour of this Legislature, but the honour of this Dominion is involved in the duty of tracing out and punishing the monster who has been guilty of this foul deed. [Hear, hear.]

Mr. STUART CAMPBELL said: I cannot allow this opportunity to pass without a few observations. It affords me painful gratification to find that, although on some occasions, I may differ from other representatives of the provinces from which I come. On this occasion, we are one in feeling, in heart, and sympathy the same, and, Sir, I feel assured that when the fatal intelligence which has bowed us almost to the dust reaches the province of which I am a representative, that there will be in that province weeping and mourning, and lamentation. Sir, the Honourable Gentleman whose death we are mourning, was well known in that province. He had there secured many warm and sincerely attached friends, not only of one class, but of all classes, and at this moment when the painful intelligence has reached that country, I feel convinced that from highest to lowest they will accord with us in the expression of the sympathy and feeling that has been made to-day. I have had no very long personal acquaintance with the illustrious dead; but I have been careful to observe his patriotic endeavours to serve the country in which his lot was cast. But if there was nothing else which he has left us as a legacy by which to remember him, the exhibition of his eloquence, of his patriotism, of his philosophy, of his kindness of heart which he displayed on the floor last night, must ever endear him to our memories and to the memories of all. I fear that the record of his sentiments last night will not be adequately preserved, I wish they could be preserved in the archives of this country, and treasured up in the hearts of the people of this land. There was sound philosophy, there was good advice addressed to the Province from which I come,—I feel there will be bequeathed to that people, a legacy of which they will be glad to avail themselves, and which in the future history of the country, will not be without extensive servitude. I am glad to hear that it is the intention of Government to take care of those who are left, I will not say to the charity, but to the justice of this House. I shall not say anything more. Those who are gifted with eloquence have felt unable to express themselves on this occasion. I can only cordially agree with the motion to adjourn this House.

The house adjourned at five minutes past four until Tuesday next.

Mr. McGee's remains were taken to Montreal, to be interred, with great pomp, at the cost of the city he represented so wisely and so well. What would have been his forty-third birthday, viz., the 13th April, 1868, will be the day of his burial. KYRIE ELEISON. May he receive the mercy for which he so often prayed !